T0129232

JAMES LOGAN, ARIZONA RANGER

J. D. LOGUE

iUniverse®

JAMES LOGAN, ARIZONA RANGER

iUniverse books may be ordered through booksellers or by contacting:

iUniverse
1663 Liberty Drive
Bloomington, IN 47403
www.iuniverse.com
1-800-Authors (1-800-288-4677)

ISBN: 978-1-5320-7982-5 (sc)
ISBN: 978-1-5320-7987-0 (e)

Library of Congress Control Number: 2019911179

Print information available on the last page.

iUniverse rev. date: 08/02/19

PROLOGUE

The Arizona Rangers are a proud law-enforcement agency whose members are committed to lives of public service. Regardless of how difficult or dangerous a situation is, Arizona Rangers have always answered the call of duty.

The company was established in 1860, but due to lack of funds, its existence was short-lived and the group was disbanded in 1882. It was reestablished in 1901 when a legislative act authorized the organization and financing of the company when Nathan Oakes Murphy was the governor.

At that time, the rangers comprised a captain (Mossman), who was paid $120 a month, a sergeant, who was paid $75 a month, and twelve privates, who were paid $55 a month.

Rynning become the second captain in 1902. Ranger James Logan, one of the privates, had to supply his own gun and horse, but $55 a month was more than a man could earn at other jobs. A farmworker or a store clerk could expect to earn $15 a month. This was a time when a gallon of milk cost 10¢ and loaf of bread 5¢, and a nice new home would have cost between $7,000 and $10,000.

CHAPTER 1

One day in 1902, Jim Logan arrived in Tombstone with a murderer. It had taken him three weeks and four days to find the person he had been looking for and eleven days on the trail to bring him back.

At night, Jim had chained him to a tree and slept with one eye open. He stopped in front of the ranger station, dismounted, and helped the murderer off his horse. The prisoner was put in a cell, and his shackles were removed. Jim went to the sergeant's office to report the details of the arrest.

After he completed the paperwork, he took his horse to the stables and chatted to it about having brought the murderer back and how difficult the cold camps and the shortage of water had been. Jim paid the groom to feed and water his horse. "Don't worry, Mr. Ranger," the groom said. "I'll take good care of your horse."

Logan removed his saddlebags, his .44-40 rifle, and his bedroll. He went across the street and asked for an upstairs room at the

Palace Saloon, the only hotel in town. Although initially reluctant to give him a room because he was certain there would be a shootout, the desk clerk relented and gave him a room in the back, where they would be less noise from the gambling hall downstairs.

Jim lit the kerosene lamp and took a clean shirt, trousers, socks, and underwear out of his bedroll. He left the room locking the door behind him and headed to the bathhouse on the boardwalk. He paid 50¢ for a towel, soap, a bath, a shave, and a haircut. He donned his clean clothes and went back to the Palace Saloon, where he had a warm beer.

He returned to his room; he had left the lamp lit to ensure he would not have to enter a dark room. He removed his boots with spurs and his trousers, and he fell onto his bed for some much-needed sleep.

The next morning, Logan went downstairs for bacon and coffee before reporting to the rangers' station for his next assignment. The captain told him that as it was Friday, he could have the weekend off and report back on Monday. The only people Jim knew in Tombstone were other rangers, but he thanked the captain and confirmed that he would see him on Monday.

He went to the stable, where he was pleased to find the groom rubbing down his horse with a curry comb and damp cloth. He also noticed that his horse had water and food. He put his saddle on a saddle rack and spent the better part of an hour cleaning it and the bridle. About noon, he left the stable and walked down the street to a restaurant. He went in and saw a counter and six tables covered with red and white checked cloths. He sat at a table facing the door. A waitress came to take his order, and he asked for a T-bone steak, mashed potatoes, and gravy. While he was waiting, he ate some hot biscuits dripping with butter and drank coffee. The steak was delicious; he decided to eat only at that place in Tombstone.

After his meal, Jim went back to the Palace Saloon, where he sat outside enjoying the warm sun. He had his feet on the hitching rail with his hat pulled down over his eyes and was half-asleep when another ranger sat beside him and asked, "How do you like being on the trail?"

"It's all right," Jim replied. "I love camping out and campfire food."

"I'm not happy with my job because I'm stuck at the office," said the other ranger.

The two enjoyed the sunshine and watching people go by.

At three, Jim got out of his chair and told his fellow ranger that he would see him in the office on Monday. He went back to the restaurant and had coffee and a piece of apple pie; he told himself that if he carried on eating like that, he would get fat. He went to his room for a nap and did not wake up until seven, when it was getting dark. The restaurant was closed, so he had a snack with a warm beer in the bar.

At nine, he went back upstairs. Because he had had the afternoon nap, he could not sleep, so he broke down his pistol, cleaned it, reassembled it, and reloaded it; he put it back in its holster. He also cleaned, oiled, and reloaded his rifle. He went to sleep about midnight.

At six the next morning, he contemplated the day ahead not knowing what to do on a Sunday in Tombstone. He wondered what his next assignment would be.

He got dressed and went to the restaurant, where he sat at the same table. The waitress took his order for hotcakes, eggs, and bacon, and when she returned with his meal, Jim exclaimed, "My goodness! I don't think I can eat all that."

"You're a big man, so you need a big meal," replied the waitress.

As he walked back to the hotel after breakfast, he saw some

rangers sitting outside the station, some of whom he knew. Ranger Bill Cody introduced Jim to the rangers he did not know, and they shared tall tales. He felt relieved that the weekend was coming to an end and that he would receive an assignment the next morning.

Jim was at the station at seven the next morning; the captain arrived, and he asked Jim to come into his office. He told Jim that his assignment would involve going to Sales, Arizona. "It's about a six-day ride. You are to arrest a murderer from Texas," the captain said. "He's a bad one, so you'll have to be on your guard from the moment you enter the town. Go to the general store next door and buy food, ammunition, and anything else you might need for this assignment. Tell the store owner to bill the Arizona Rangers. I'll see you when you return with that murderer, Texas Red."

"Yes sir," Jim said. He went to the store for a small slab of bacon, a one-pound sack of flour, a pound of sugar, five pounds of oats for his horse, and salt and pepper. In addition, he brought a sack of hardtack, two boxes of .44 ammunition, one box of .45 ammunition, three boxes of .44-70 rifle ammunition, and a canteen that was larger than the one he had.

He went to the stable to get organized for his assignment. He saddled his horse having made sure there were no wrinkles in the blanket under the saddle. He attached his bedroll to the saddle and did the same with his saddlebags, which held the items he had bought. His last task before he led his horse outside was to secure his .44-70 in its scabbard.

Back at the station, he loaded up the rest of his supplies and checked to make sure everything was tied down and secure. He chatted with some of the rangers who were sitting outside, and he learned from the sergeant that there was no further information about the man he was to arrest and bring back for a trial. Jim told the sergeant and the other rangers there that he would be back in two or three weeks. He went out, mounted his horse, and rode down the main street stirring up dust as he went.

That night as he camped under the stars, Jim thought he was in heaven; he enjoyed nothing more than sleeping out in the wild. Before the sun came up, he put wood on the fire and put water on to make coffee. He fried some bacon and had some hardtack with his coffee. He cleaned up the campsite and put out the fire. After saddling his horse and making sure he had secured all his supplies, he set off before daylight.

Having not seen anyone all morning, he arrived at a small town of Mescal at noon, where he decided to stop and eat. The residents there found out that Jim was a ranger, and they asked him to take a Mexican who had murdered his wife to jail in Tucson. Jim told them that he was not going to Tucson but that he would take the prisoner to Agua Linda.

After lunch, Jim checked on the prisoner to see whether he had been beaten up or had sustained a gunshot wound. The prisoner was fit enough to be taken to Agua Linda. The townspeople made a horse available. Jim and the prisoner rode off. He told Jim that his name was Pedro, but he preferred to be called Pete.

It would be a three-day ride to Agua Linda. Jim told Pete, "If you do right by me, I'll do right by you, but if you don't, this ride'll be bad for you."

That night, they set up camp. After Jim hobbled the horses and made a fire, they had a meal of hardtack and coffee. Jim removed Pete's handcuffs so that he could eat and relieve himself, but then he cuffed him in a way that allowed him to move around but only slowly.

Jim did not sleep much that night as he knew that if Pete tried to escape, it would be during the first night.

Pete got up around four in the morning and noticed that the

ranger was not asleep. He stoked the fire and added some wood before going back to sleep.

The ranger got up at five thirty and made breakfast—the rest of the bacon and coffee. They had to eat the bacon; with no refrigeration or salting, it would not have kept for four days.

Jim washed the dishes, poured the remainder of the coffee on the campfire, and cleaned up the camp area. He and Pete saddled the horses and were on their way at daybreak.

That morning passed uneventfully; they never saw anyone, and they did not talk. They stopped at a small creek at one. They took the saddles off the horses and the pack off the pack horse and let them drink at the stream. After the men ate some hardtack and rested for a while, they saddled the horses and put the pack back on the pack horse.

Their ride in the afternoon passed in much the same way; they rode without seeing another person until evening. As the sun was going down, they came upon a thicket of white oak trees where they decided to camp for the night.

After they had seen to the horses and hobbled them, Jim shot a jackrabbit and cooked it. They sat around the fire in the cool of the night. Jim asked Pete, "How long have you been in Arizona?"

"My wife, my two children, and I moved here in 1889."

"What'll happen to your children with both parents gone?" Jim asked, but Pete did not reply.

When they were getting ready to turn in for the night, Jim handcuffed Pete in the same way as he had the previous night. When he bent down to secure the other handcuffs, Pete, with all his strength, pushed the saddle into the ranger and knocked him off balance. He tried to overpower Jim and run, but Jim pulled his .44 Colt and shot three times. Pete was dead before he hit the ground. The ranger looked down at the lifeless body. "You son of a dog. Why did you do that? You knew I'd shoot you."

Because Pete's body would be stiff by the morning, Jim laid him out straight and fell into a sound sleep realizing he did not need to feel guilty or ashamed for having done his duty. If he had let Pete get away, who knows how many others he could have harmed?

The next morning, Jim rose while it was still dark. He broke camp, saddled the horses, and tied Pete over the back of the second horse. With only brief stops to rest the horses, Jim rode on until he arrived in Agua Linda, where he handed Pete's body over to the sheriff. He completed the paperwork detailing how Pete had died.

Jim carried on toward Sells, Arizona. His assignment was to find the outlaw and escort him to a place a hundred and ten miles west of Tombstone, where the man would stand trial for shooting eleven men over several years. In Phoenix, the ranger had bought a .45 Buntline Peacemaker gun, and when he stopped for lunch, he tried it out. It was a little heavier than what he was used to, but it was well balanced and did not have the strong kick that his .44 Peacemaker had. He realized he was spending too much time on his new toy. He put the Buntline in his saddlebags and carried on.

On the third day, he arrived in Sell and noted two people coming toward him, but the sun was in his eyes and he could not see them clearly. He was worried that they were people who wanted to stop him from carrying out his assignment or were members of the Texan's gang, who were known to have been working in the saloon. However, as the people drew nearer, Jim saw that they were just a husband and wife on their way home. They greeted each other, but the ranger heard the woman whisper to her husband, "Don't look at him. Someone with such a big gun on his hip must be an outlaw on the run!"

The horse must have sensed Jim's tension because when a tumbleweed blew across the road, it shied and almost threw Jim out of the saddle. He calmed the horse down by rubbing his neck and speaking softly to it. Encountering no further incidents on his way into town, Jim went straight to the stable. The groomer asked whether the ranger had come from Tombstone. "Yes I have," said Jim. "I'm with the Arizona Rangers. I won't be in town too long. I've come to take an outlaw who murdered eleven people in Texas back to Tombstone. I'll see that he gets to jail in Tombstone dead or alive."

"Good luck, ranger," said the groom.

Jim walked down the street looking for accommodations and saw a place that advertised rooms for rent. He went in and saw everyone in the dining room having their midday meal.

"Do you have a room to rent?" Jim asked the silver-haired landlady.

"Yes," she said. "I have rooms to rent by the day, week, or month. Twenty-five cents a day for the room, and twenty-five cents a day for food—in advance. What would you like?"

"By the day," Jim said. "I don't know how long I'll be here. And I would like meals."

He paid for two days and was told that breakfast was from six to nine, the noon meal was from noon to one, and dinner was from five thirty to six thirty. The landlady led Jim upstairs. "Do you have a room at the back?" he asked.

"I have one that looks out over the backyard," the landlady replied.

When they got to the room, he opened the windows as the room was stuffy. He put his personal items down and asked, "Can you feed me today? If not, I'll go to a saloon for a sandwich."

The landlady fed him, and when he was finished eating, he stepped outside and looked up and down the street. He wondered where the outlaw would be.

It wasn't long before the outlaw got word that an Arizona

ranger was in town looking for him. He declared that he wasn't concerned as other law enforcement officials had tried to take him back to Texas before and had not succeeded. "This Arizona ranger will just be one more notch on my gun. I'm not going back to Texas."

It was at ten past four in the afternoon when they faced each other in the street. The Texas killer had a Colt .44 at his right side and a small .25 caliber handgun in his vest pocket. His plan was to act as though he was going to use the .44 and while his opponent was watching his right hand, he would shoot him with the belly gun with his left hand. That was how he had managed to kill fourteen men: two law enforcers, a sheriff, and the eleven men in Texas. As far as Texas Red was concerned, the ranger would just be one more law enforcer who had tried to arrest him and had failed.

Jim said, "I'm an Arizona ranger, and I'm here to take you back to Tombstone. Whether I take you dead or alive is up to you."

Jim had made sure that the sun was behind him and therefore in the eyes of the Texas outlaw. As he had done before, the outlaw made as though he was going for his .44 but went for his .25. Four shots rang out. The outlaw had not cleared leather before he was fatally shot four times. He collapsed thirty-five feet from the ranger. The outlaw had learned too late that the ranger's aim was deadly with that big gun. The residents of that town talk about the fastest ranger who had come to their town for a long time.

The ranger walked over to the Texan on the ground. He searched his pockets and handed the money he found to the undertaker saying, "Give him a good funeral." He turned to those who had witnessed the death of the Texan. "Please write down everything that happened here and bring your reports to the boardinghouse where I'm staying. I'll be returning to Tombstone tomorrow."

By the time the body had been taken to the funeral parlor, he received written statements from six witnesses.

The landlady gave him his evening meal and told him she would be sorry to see him leave. "I hope you have a trouble-free journey, and if you're ever back here, be sure and stop by."

In his room, he packed his .45. He wondered if he should exchange it for his .44, but when he looked at the long barrel, he decided against it. He realized that the one he had would be better if he had to draw and shoot fast.

He packed and was all ready for his departure in the morning. After a good night's sleep, he got up at five-thirty and went to the stable. He paid the groomer before saddling his horse and securing his bedroll, saddlebags, and .44-70 Winchester rifle.

It was early in the morning when the ranger mounted his horse and starting the ride back to Tombstone for new orders. He took in his surroundings as he rode. It was a dry landscape—no trees, just patches of grass and tumbleweeds.

Jim followed his familiar routine of setting up camp in the evening, eating, and sleeping under the stars, which he loved. After breakfast, he would clean up camp and be on his way before daylight.

He had no trouble on the eight-day journey back to Tombstone. He reported to Captain Rynning, who said, "You've done a good job. Take the weekend off. Come in on Monday. I have another job for you."

Jim led his horse to the stable and paid the groomer to give the animal a rubdown and extra grain and water. He asked the groomer if there were any new and good-looking women on the scene. Jim was not surprised when the groomer replied in the negative. He went to the Palace Saloon and got a room upstairs and in the back, away from the noise. He unpacked and took a change of clothes to the bathhouse, where he had a bath and a shave.

Feeling decent once more, he went to the Palace Saloon for a warm beer and some snacks. He went back to the hotel and sat on the veranda; he almost fell asleep in the warm sun.

About five, he walked to the ranger station, where some rangers were sitting around and chatting. Jim joined them, and they talked about the rangers who had been killed in the line of duty and in their private lives.

Around ten thirty, everyone began leaving, and Jim went up to his room.

After a lazy Sunday, Jim went to the station bright and early on Monday morning. The captain said, "I have a job for you. I'll tell you about it, and you can decline it if you want. The job is to fetch Hanes, who's up in the Hopi Indian reservation north of Flagstaff. He's the head of the Hanes gang from Pratt, Kansas, but we don't know what they're doing way out here. This is a tough job and will take a long time."

"When do you want me to leave?" Jim asked.

"Today if you can."

"I'm ready to go. I'll fetch my horse and gear."

"Go to the dry goods store and draw enough supplies for two weeks. Put it on the rangers' bill."

Jim fetched his horse and gear and went to the store for beans, rice, hardtack, a sack of sugar, eggs, a sack of salt, and a sack of oats for his horse. His last stop was at the ranger station, where he was given money for a train ticket from Tucson to Flagstaff and the arrest warrants. With a farewell to the rangers who were sitting in the sun outside the station, he mounted his horse and rode out of town on his way to Tucson. He camped out under the stars as he liked to.

He got up in the morning, had breakfast, and checked the campsite. He put his tack on his horse and set off before it was light. It was hot as he rode; with every step, the horse kicked up little clouds of dust. Jim thought that they were in need of some rain. He pushed on as fast as he could stopping to give his horse a rest only once in a while. By the time he rode into the town of Mescal, where he had picked up Pete, it was after dark. The groomer in the stable asked him, "Ranger, are you after someone around here?"

"No," said Jim. "I'm just passing through on my way to Tucson. Where can I get a room for the night?" The groomer directed Jim to accommodations down the street, where he got a room and breakfast for 50¢. He put his gear on top of the bed and slept.

He went down to breakfast the next morning and fetched his horse. It was after eight before he was on his way again. During the day, he saw a few riders on the road. He stopped to rest his horse, and he arrived in Tucson around nine that night. He arranged to stable his horse for at least two weeks and wrapped his .44-70 Winchester in his bedroll. He took his saddlebags with him.

He went to the station. His train was leaving in two hours, so he went to the bar for a meal. When the train arrived, the ranger was the last to board because he waited for the women and children as well as the men with wives to be seated. He was pleasantly surprised to see how well appointed the train was with pretty lace curtains.

Jim put his feet up on the empty seat opposite him and tried to relax. It was after midnight when the train arrived in Flagstaff, so Jim waited in the stable's livery room until morning. When the groomer came in, Jim told the man, "I need a good, strong horse. It doesn't have to be fast, but it needs to have enough stamina for a long ride."

After Jim chose a horse, the groomer saddled it and gave him a bag of grain, which he put in his saddlebags. He put the Winchester on the side of the saddle and checked his saddlebags.

Jim mounted the horse and said, "Damn. This Morgan is a big horse. If he were any taller, I'd have to use a box to mount him." Jim told the groomer, "I'm going to Kayenta in the Hopi reservation. My business may take two weeks, but I'm hoping I'll be back sooner than that."

"Kayenta is on the Navajo reservation, not on the Hopi," the groomer said. "It's in the northeast corner of Arizona, and it'll take you a good week just to get there. Also, there isn't much water on the way."

It was a good hundred and fifty miles from Flagstaff to Kayenta, and it took the ranger ten days to get there. He was very pleased that the Morgan did not seem to be tired from the long journey. Despite being hot and thirsty, he was concerned for his horse, so he took the Morgan to the stable and paid the groomer to feed and water it.

He asked the groomer, "Do you know Red Hanes? Is he working someplace around here? I'd like to see him before I go back to Pratt because we worked together in Kansas."

"I don't know him, but people come and go all the time."

"Where's a good place to get the room here in town?"

"Mrs. Brown has a boardinghouse down the street, and she puts on a good meal," the groomer said.

Jim thanked him and went to Mrs. Brown's boardinghouse, where he rented a room for a week. He told her that he was not sure how long he would be staying as he was looking for someone. Mrs. Brown told the ranger that meals were 25¢ a day. As it was after one, Jim went to the bar for a meal and returned to the boardinghouse at about three thirty.

That night at dinner, he found himself sitting next to a pretty redhead, Sara MacDonald. She looked to be in her twenties and was the town's schoolteacher. They talked for a long time; she had been teaching in Kayenta Township for four years.

After Sara said good evening and went to her room, Jim went to the saloon for a beer, the only one he drank all night. When he asked the people in the saloon whether anyone knew Red Hanes, a man said, "I know a redheaded man, but his name isn't Hanes, it's Hendershot."

"Does he work around here?"

"He has a place about two miles south of town."

The next day, Jim went to the stable, saddled his horse, and rode out to the Hendershot Ranch to see whether Hendershot was Hanes. As he approached the ranch, he noticed nine horses in the corral—not a good sign. In front of the house, he shouted, "Hello!"

A woman with two children come to the door and asked. "What do you need? How can I help you?"

Jim said, "I'm from Pratt, Kansas, and would like to see Red before I go back."

"Red won't be back till this afternoon. Get off your horse."

Jim dismounted and went into the house. The woman asked, "Would you like some water?" She turned to one of the children. "Joe, take his horse to the water." The boy led the horse to the water tank, but the horse would not drink. Another woman and three more children came out with some cold water, and the group sat outside in some shade.

The first woman asked, "How do you know Red?"

"We worked together in Pratt."

Around two thirty, a redheaded man came to the house and introduced himself. When Jim realized he was not Red Hanes, he came clean and confessed to lying to the family. He told them he was looking for an outlaw named Hanes, who was somewhere in the area. The women accepted his apology. Mr. Hendershot said, "I haven't seen a redheaded man for over a year. People said he went back to Kansas. I don't know if that's right or not."

The ranger thanked them for their help, mounted his horse, and went back to town thinking, *That was a waste of time.* Hendershot had not looked anything like the picture of Red Hanes that had been on the flyer.

He stopped at the stables, removed his saddle and bridle, and fed and watered his horse. He put his saddlebags over his shoulder and went to the saloon for a beer. A card game was going on in the back. The ranger looking over the people playing and thought, *Damn! The person I've been looking for is right over there playing cards!* He went up to him and said, "Red Hanes, I've been looking for you. I'm an Arizona ranger, and I've come to take you to jail."

Red Hanes jumped up with a gun in his hand and managed to fire one shot before the ranger returned fire. Six shots were fired. Red was still standing, but one round had struck the ranger in the arm. The ranger pulled the Buntline Peacemaker out of the saddlebags and pulled the trigger twice. The outlaw dropped to the floor but was not dead. The ranger said to the onlookers, "Get a doctor."

Holding his wounded arm, Jim sat. When the doctor come, the outlaw was taken out, and the doctor looked at Jim's arm. "Come to my office. I'll take the bullet out and clean your wound." Before he left, Jim asked the bystanders to write down what they had just witnessed.

While the doctor was treating him, Jim asked about the outlaw and was told that he had been hit five times—twice in a leg, once in an arm, and twice in the stomach. Also, one ear was missing, and he had a bad cut on his forehead. Jim was concerned when the doctor said, "He won't be able to be moved for a long time. It'll take months if not years before he recovers."

The ranger went to the stable to fetch his .44-70 Winchester before going to the boardinghouse. The groom told the ranger that some of Hanes's friends would be looking for him. The ranger sent a telegram to Captain Rynning explaining what had happened and asking what he should do. The captain's reply was that a law enforcer would be arriving from Liberal, Kansas, in ten days and that the outlaws should be turned over to him. The captain told him that if all went to plan, he should return to Tombstone. He told Jim to do whatever he felt was best. Jim confirmed these plans with the sheriff, and the sheriff said he would keep Hanes.

As Jim was going back to his room, two men stepped in front of him and said, "We're calling you out because you shot Red. We're here to settle the score and stand up for him."

Jim could use only one arm, but he drew his gun and said, "Drop your guns and turn around." One did what he was told, but the other moved his hand down to his gun. The ranger said, "Drop it or use it!" The man dropped his gun, put his hands up, and turned his back to the ranger.

"Let's all take a walk to the sheriff's office," said the ranger. When they walked into the office, Jim asked the sheriff, "Are they a part of the Kansas bunch? They stopped me and said they were going to shoot me, but there sporting blood turned to horse hockey. Luckily for them, they turned over their guns and came in. Otherwise, they'd be dead by now."

After the men were put in cells, the sheriff asked, "Would you like a cup of coffee?"

"Yes, that would be good."

"Where are you staying?"

"Mrs. Brown's boardinghouse."

"Mrs. Brown provides good meals."

At dinner that night, Jim got to know the other people staying at the boardinghouse and learned more about Sara MacDonald, whom he had met the night before. She was twenty, five-two, and weighed about 110. She had red hair and green eyes; Jim considered her a very nice-looking woman. They had coffee, and she told him about herself and how she had become a schoolteacher. She had been born in Ohio; she had graduated in the top half of her class. When her brother became the Indian representative of the Navajo in 1901, she was eighteen. She saw no future for herself in Ohio, so she packed up and went to live in Arizona with her brother on the reservation. She was appointed by the board of representatives of the Navajo tribe as a teacher. She taught all the children from first to eighth grade in a one-room school.

At breakfast the next day, Jim asked her, "Can I walk you to the school?"

Sara agreed, and on Sunday, they went to Sunday school together.

At about four that afternoon, Jim received a note from the doctor telling him that Red had died at eleven that morning. Jim said, "Sara, my job is over here, so I'll be going back to Tombstone."

She said that it had been good meeting him and that if he ever came that way again, he should look her up.

The next morning, he had coffee with Sara, who kissed him goodbye. He rode out of town heading south toward Flagstaff. He arrived nine days later and turned his horse back in to the stable. He told the groomer that he would be paid for providing such a good horse.

He got a room for the night, and the next day, he took the train to Tucson; he arrived after dark.

The next day, he paid for the room he had taken for the night and went to fetch his horse from the stable. It had been a long journey for the ranger. He rode the whole of the first day and camped out in the cold. The next morning, he started off again without breakfast or coffee. He rode all morning and saw no one except a couple in a buckboard.

At noon, he arrived in Mescal. He had come to like that town; the people were friendly and would go out of their way to help others. He had dinner there, and the storekeeper asked, "How are you doing?"

"I'm doing fine," Jim said. "No more bad guys at the moment. I'm on my way back to Tombstone, where I'll be given new orders. I wonder what hellhole I'll be going to next."

The ranger headed out of town toward Tombstone. On the way, his thoughts turned to Sara and her flaming red hair and green eyes that seemed to see right through him. He thought of the possibility of their getting married. He wondered what kind of life they would have with his going all over Arizona to get bad guys and take them to jail.

About a half hour before sunset, he stopped and set up camp for the night. He removed the saddle and bridle from his horse and hobbled it. He carried the saddlebags to the campfire. He had shot a jackrabbit, which he cooked with rice and beans. The night was cool. He put his sleeping bag close to the fire and went to sleep.

CHAPTER 2

When Ranger James Logan reported to Captain Rynning at the rangers' headquarters for new orders, he was informed that the headquarters was moving to Tucson; the reason for this was to improve service by being close to the train station. "We can be in any town in Arizona in just two days," the captain explained.

All the rangers who were not out on assignments helped with moving the office to Tucson, and it was up and running within a week. Jim has been a ranger for just over five years. His new orders were to go to the sheriff in Flagstaff and bring a man back to headquarters. He went to Flagstaff and brought the man back the next night.

On October 23, 1904, four regulars were on duty at the Palace Saloon—the bartender, the craps dealer, the roulette dealer, and a reporter—as well as some customers. Just before midnight, Joe Bostwick came in through the back door with a red bandanna over his face with holes cut for his eyes. He was brandishing a long-barrel Colt .45. "Hands up!" he ordered. He did not notice Breeder, a customer, slipping out the front door.

Outside, Breeder spotted an officer wearing a Arizona Rangers star that was sparkling in the moonlight. It was Jim, who was coming from the restaurant. "Don't go in there," Breeder said when the ranger headed toward the saloon. "There's a holdup going on in there."

"All right, that's what I am here for." Jim pulled out his .45 single-action Colt and stepped through the front door. Bostwick turned and fired at him but missed. The ranger's first shot hit Bostwick just above the right eye. Bostwick fired wildly. The ranger fired once more, that time hitting Bostwick in the chest. He collapsed to the floor.

The next day when he was interviewed by a reporter from the *Tucson Citizen*, Jim commented, "I'm sorry this happened, but if I hadn't been faster on the draw than he was, I might be in his position." The reporter asked him what he had seen. Jim replied, "It was all over before I had a chance to think about it. I gave him a chance to put down his weapon, but he fired at me and I returned the fire."

Back at the rangers' headquarters, the captain asked Jim, "How would you like to have your own office in Flagstaff? You could mail in your reports, and if necessary, you could telephone me. You'd cover the area from the state lines in the west, north, and south. You'll be on the go all the time, but we can send you help if you need it."

"Will I get paid more?"

"Yes. You'll receive a sergeant's pay—seventy-five dollars a month."

Jim was happy to hear all of that. "When do you need me in the office in Flagstaff?"

"In two or three weeks. Do you think you'll need more time?"

"No," Jim said. "That'll be enough time for me to have the office up and running."

The next morning, Jim and two other rangers put their horses in the cattle car of a train headed to Flagstaff. One ranger was called High Pockets as he was six-seven. David was not tall, only five-six, but he weighed 175. In Flagstaff, they would need somewhere to stay, a good place to eat, and stables.

The got there at three in the afternoon. They went to the office to see what work needed to be done. The walls of the jail were adobe, and the windows needed bars. Two sides of the cell block also needed bars, and they needed to build a wall closing it off from the office. Other than that, the building was fine.

It wasn't long before they got their first job—two ranchers were shooting at each other, so Jim sent High Pockets and Dave to sort it out. They got the two ranchers to calm down and agree to stop shooting at one another, and all returned to normal.

Jim couldn't stop thinking about Sara. It was a three-day ride to Kayenta, so he would have to take at least a week off to see her. But then someone told him that the train stopped in Chitc'shbito, which was only twenty-five miles from Kayenta. "I usually go and come back in a weekend," the man told Jim.

After their first payday, Jim told the other rangers that he was going to Kayenta and would be back in two or three days. He got the train and was in Chitc'shbito in just four hours. He got his horse out of the cattle car and headed to Kayenta. It was afternoon when he got to the school, and he waited outside.

When Sara came out to lock the school door, Jim said, "Hi, Sara."

Sara turned around surprised. "Jim! I didn't think I'd ever see you again. Thank God you've come back. It's good to see you." She kissed him.

"It's good to see you," he said and kissed her back. "I've been thinking about you and missing you, so now that I had some time off, I've come to see you."

Sara said, "Let's go to the boardinghouse."

The next day, Saturday, Jim and Sara had a picnic and realized they were falling in love. That night, he went to heaven in her room.

On Sunday, he said, "I have to leave at eleven in the morning so I can catch the train back to Flagstaff."

"When will you come back to see me?"

"I don't know, Sara. I have a ranger office to run. How about you come to see me? When school is out, do you think you could come? If you can get to Chitc'shbito, you can catch the train to Flagstaff. The train takes four hours, but from here to Chitc'shbito is a five-hour ride on horseback. There's someone at the office twenty-four hours a day seven days a week. They may be sleeping in one of the cells, but there's always someone there, and they'll let me know. Will you come?"

"I don't know. I've never been on a train before. Yes! I'll come to Flagstaff."

Jim took her in his arm and asked, "Will you be my wife?"

"Yes, I'll marry you even though we haven't known each other for very long."

Jim told Sara that she could take her horse on the train. "If they say no, tell them Ranger Logan said you needed to bring that horse to Flagstaff. They'll get it on the train for you."

Sara said, "Jim, we'll soon be husband and wife forever. I'll come as soon as school is out, but that will feel like a lifetime!"

"I'll get us a house and furniture. We'll need crockery, cutlery, pots, and pans too. I'll do that by the time school's out. By the time you come, you'll have a place you can call home." He kissed her and mounted his horse. "I don't know when I'll be able to come back, but if I get some time off before school's out, I'll come and see you."

At the train station, he saw a Navajo husband and wife. He

boarded the train and was back in Flagstaff in no time. He went to the office; Dave caught Jim up with all that had been going on. He looked through all the paperwork and the new wanted posters. By the time he was finished, it was after midnight; he was too tired to go to the boardinghouse, so he slept in a cell.

He was up and about by six the next morning. He cleaned the grease and grime from his .45 Peacemaker, reloaded it, and put it in his holster. That afternoon, he went to the boardinghouse for a shower and a shave and a change of clothes.

The next day, they received a flyer about an outlaw who was being released from prison and would be coming to Flagstaff. Jim said, "Maybe he's an old man who just wants to come home. We'll look out for him."

They got a call from the Navajo police in Window Rock. The officer said that two white eyes had been picked up for cattle rustling; he wanted the Arizona Rangers to come and take them off their hands. Jim agreed to do that. He told Dave, "This would be a good job for High Pockets."

When High Pockets returned from patrol and had given his daily report, Logan asked him, "How would you like to go to Window Rock and bring back two prisoners the Navajo police are holding for cattle rustling?" High Pockets said, "Yes, I'd like to get out of town for a change."

He went to the rifle rack, unlocked it, and got his .44-70 Winchester and two boxes of .45 bullets for his Colt Peacemaker. He packed his gear and went to the general store for two pounds of hardtack, one pound of coffee, and a small bag of sugar. He went to the train station and bought a ticket. He loaded his horse into the cattle car and took a seat in the Pullman car.

Jim and Dave were there to see him off. "With High Pockets out of town, we'll have to put in some overtime to pick up the slack," Jim told Dave.

They found out that they couldn't manage twelve-hours shifts, so they tried working shifts of ten hours on and ten hours off. However, they realized that there wouldn't be a standard pattern and that their hours would be different each day.

The head office in Tucson sent two rangers to help out. One was six feet tall and weighed 135. His sidearm was a 1911 .45 Colt automatic and had seven rounds with one in the chamber. He had two extra clips on his belt. The other ranger, Bob, carried a German P38 with fifteen rounds, and he carried two extra clips for it. Bob was also six feet tall, but he weighed 175. With the extra manpower, they went back to three eight-hour shifts a day.

Time went by slowly for Jim; he was bored. It was still nineteen days until school was out for Sara. He did not like his new job; he felt like a storekeeper. All was quiet and peaceful, and there were no laws that needed enforcing.

At eight one evening, the ranger on duty checked that all the doors were locked and secure and did the same at eleven. The midnight watch did two rounds during that shift. Jim said, "If nothing happens in the next couple of days, I'm going to rob the bank just to stir up some activity in this dead town."

The sheriff's office took care of the drunks on Saturday night, and the rangers had not been called out in two weeks. Bob had written one speeding ticket to an out-of-state driver on Highway 66. "That's all we had to do this week," Jim said. "There hasn't even been a bar fight. It's so quiet it stinks."

Jim was in his office daydreaming about Sara, who would be coming in eighteen days, when a telegram came. Jim showed it to Carl when he returned after his rounds. Carl read it and asked, "What are you going to do about this?"

"I'm going to Window Rock and find those murdering sons of bitches. No one murders an Arizona ranger and gets away with it. I'm going to bring those murdering cattle-rustling bastards back, and if they so much as blink an eye, they'll be dead. High Pockets didn't deserve to die this way. Carl, go tell Dave that High Pockets has been murdered by the two cattle rustlers he went to pick up at the Navajo police station in Window Rock."

Jim got his .44-70 Winchester, a double-barreled shotgun, and ammunition for both. He wrote out instructions for the rangers in his absence. He was about to leave the office when Dave came in and said, "I want to go after them!"

"No. You'd kill them. We aren't in that business of murdering people."

Jim bought a train ticket to Window Rock and asked about getting a horse at the destination, but the ticket agent could not help them with that. So he got his horse and saddle from the stables and went back to the station. When the train arrived, he put the horse in the cattle car and went to the Pullman car.

It took five hours to get to Window Rock; it was three in the afternoon when Jim arrived at the Navajo police station. He picked up warrants for the arrests for cattle rustling. The paperwork for murder charges against the cattle rustlers was not yet available, so Jim asked if there was any news or whether anybody had seen or heard from them. The Navajo policeman said, "No, but we'll go out with you at daybreak tomorrow."

"That will be welcome help as you know the country," Jim replied.

At daybreak, Jim and two Navajo police officers set off after the cattle rustlers who had killed High Pockets. If they caught them, they would arrest them only for cattle rustling, but they were sure warrants for the murder of High Pockets would be issued.

Jim was still mad as hell about the murder of High Pockets. He had never killed anyone for revenge, but these two cattle rustlers might be the first.

They traveled south for fifteen miles and went in a westerly direction to pick up the trail in the wasteland area of Arizona. On the first day as they had expected, they did not see any signs of the rustlers. They camped in a dry area for the night. At sunrise, they broke camp and continued west.

On the third day, they came across the tracks of two horses going south. It was apparent that the horses had been moving fast; the tracks were a good day old. Jim removed a map from his saddlebags and saw that the town of Wellington was in that direction. The Navajo police knew what the cattle rustlers looked like and could identify them.

When they arrived in Wellington, they went into the first saloon they saw and looked around but did not see the rustlers. The police officer showed the bartender pictures of the rustlers and asked if he had seen them. The bartender said that he had not but that he worked during the day only. They decided to wait for the evening bartender, who came in at six. When he arrived, Jim asked him to look at the mugshots of the two cattle rustlers. "Have you seeing them?"

"Yes, they were in here last night. They asked me about a boardinghouse, and I told them there was a good one about twelve doors down the street."

The three of them went to the boardinghouse and showed the mugshots to the landlady; she told them they were in their rooms at the time.

Jim asked, "Are there any others in the rooms up there?"

"No, they're all at work," she said.

Jim asked for the key to the rustlers' room and told the landlady to stay downstairs as there might be shooting. With gun in hand, Jim unlocked the door and kicked it open. The two rustlers had been asleep; they were arrested without incident.

Jim would have liked them to draw their guns so he would

have had an excuse to kill them, but he realized this way was probably better—they would have to sit in jail waiting to be hanged.

When Jim and the policemen stopped for the night on the way back, they arranged to stand watch for four hours each. When they got back to the Navajo police headquarters, the rustlers were charged with the murder of High Pockets. The two Navajo policeman and the ranger took the murderers to the train station and chained them to a beam in the baggage car.

On the way back to Flagstaff, Jim told them, "I'd love it if you tried to make a break for it. I'd kill you in a heartbeat and think nothing of it. You two are lower than whale shit at the bottom of the ocean. You're lucky I'm an Arizona ranger because that's all that's keeping me from beating the hell out of you."

When the train pulled into Flagstaff, the rangers there were on the platform. According to the requirements of the state, they took the murdering cattle rustlers to John Sloan at the sheriff's office. After they had been locked in the cell, Jim said, "Back up and put your hands through the bars so I can remove your handcuffs." He unlocked the cuffs on the first man and told him to go to the other side of the cell and face the wall. He repeated the procedure with the second man. Jim signed the paperwork turning the men over to the sheriff. As he walked out of the sheriff's office, he said to the outlaws, "See you at your hanging."

Although school was out, there was no sign of Sara. Another week passed before Sara phoned Jim. She said she had just finished all the after-school work and had been getting things ready for the new teacher. She told him she would be arriving on the noon train the next day.

Early the next morning, Sara and her brother started the five-hour ride to the train station; he helped her into the train with her baggage. Four hours later, she arrived in Flagstaff. And extremely happy man fetched her from the station. Jim helped her into the wagon and drove her to their new home. He could not believe that he had fallen in love at his age—twenty-seven—and he wasn't getting any younger. Sara was young and beautiful. Just one look from her turned the rainiest day into the most beautiful sunny day.

When Jim and Sara found out they were going to have a baby, they were delighted especially when the doctor said all was looking good.

Jim went off after some robbers who had robbed the bank in Flagstaff and were then in Williams. As there were only four people involved, Jim did not need help. He stopped at the Flagstaff bank to see if the employees had anything to add to the report. At Williams, he identified himself as a ranger and asked if the men he was looking for were there. He said, "I'm going to be in town only as long as it takes me to arrest them. I'll take them back to Flagstaff today dead or alive."

The outlaws heard that an Arizona ranger was in town looking for them, but because there were four of them, they were sure they had the advantage. At four in the afternoon, they faced the ranger, who had his back to the sun, so it was in the robbers' eyes. The ranger had his old .45 Colt Peacemaker tied down on his leg, and he had his .45 Buntline in his belt. One of the outlaws said, "You must be nuts. There are four of us and just one of you."

Jim said, "I'll have you know that today you're coming back to Flagstaff with me on the charges of robbing a bank. Whether you're dead or alive is up to you."

One robber said, "Show me your warrants."

"I have them right here. I suggest you drop those gun belts if you want to see the sun rise tomorrow. If you don't, you'll be going to Flagstaff tied to the back of your horses. It's up to you."

One of the outlaws put his hand on his gun. The ranger

said, "Go on, pull that hogleg. You'll be dead before you hit the ground. The rest of you, remove your guns and put them down." All four dropped their gun belts. The ranger said, "You've made a good choice. I would have killed you in a heartbeat."

Jim handcuffed them without having to pull his gun. Jim told them they would be leaving for Flagstaff the next day. Because there was no jail in Williams, Jim and the stableman guarded them that night.

The next day at sunup, they were on the road to Flagstaff and got there late in the afternoon. They had stopped to eat, and the ranger had checked that their handcuffs were not cutting into them. They pulled up in front of the sheriff's office, dismounted, and went inside. The sheriff put them in cells. Jim went to his office and told the rangers that the bank robbers were in custody at the sheriff's office.

When Jim arrived at his home, he saw that a midwife was looking after Sara. She told them not to worry as the baby was not due for another two weeks. It had been just a false alarm. She said, "I'll see you in a couple of weeks."

Jim had to go north of Flagstaff to find bad guys who had taken twenty horses. When he caught up with them, they offered no resistance, and he took the whole gang to Flagstaff. When he arrived home, he discovered that Sara had given birth and all was well.

Jim felt that his job had changed. He was no longer dealing with train robbers, cattle rustlers, or bank robbers. There were no long days on the trail and camping out under the stars, which he loved, because there was a train station in town. The state had given the Flagstaff rangers a Model T Ford that replaced their horses. Jim would send junior officers out after lawbreakers while he stayed in Flagstaff. He hated that; he felt he had become just a glorified bookkeeper.

Some of the new recruits had come from the New Mexico mounted police, and one of their group had been killed in a gunfight on October 8, 1907. Jefferson "Jeff" P. Kidder was killed in a shootout in the town of Nacho Sonora on April 8, 1908. They had both died in the line of duty.

One of Captain Rynning's most notable recruits was Sergeant Jeff Averett. He was an expert pistol shot who practiced intensively with his gun and was normally based in Nogales. On New Year's Eve in 1906, Averett was sent to Douglas to help control some troublemakers. Two rangers were patrolling near the railroad roundhouse and encountered a saloonkeeper coming out of the back door and staggering across the tracks. Ranger Jeff shouted, "Hold on there! We want to look at you." Woods broke into a run and turned and shot at the ranger. Jeff quickly pulled his .45 Colt and fired three shots.

Another ranger, James T. Holmes, "Shorty," was stationed at Roosevelt. On October 31, 1905, he went after Bernardo Arviso, a bootlegger suspected of selling to the Indians. When the bootlegger fired at him, the ranger fired back killing the bootlegger. While he never sustained a gunshot wound, Shorty put more outlaws in the ground than he put in jail. He was cited for distinguished service in 1906 and 1907.

Wheeler was the son of a West Point graduate, a colonel in the US Army. Wheeler joined the Arizona Rangers in 1903. In June 1907, he tracked someone who had escaped from the Yuma jail for five days on horseback through the desert. Wheeler, Johnny Cameron, the sheriff, and two Indian guides rode for thirty miles in blistering heat. The water in their canteens was so hot that they couldn't drink it, and the glare of the sun on the sand was unbearable. The horses went without water.

The next day, the Indian guide found the outlaws' camp about three miles east of a mining settlement. They were asleep, and there were six horses hobbled nearby. The ranger and the sheriff closed in. Wheeler called out, "You're surrounded. Give up in the name of the law."

These were just a few of the rangers Jim could remember offhand. There had been so many others through the years Jim knew personally. One was David Gillespie, who had been shot three times by a Thompson .45 machine gun at a roadblock in Flagstaff.

CHAPTER 3

Jim did not like the fact that his job had changed into an office job. There was no more camping out; he could take trains and get to his destination within hours instead of days.

The people had also changed. The new rangers were no longer carrying old .45 Colts; they had new 1911 .45 automatic Colts, and some had 9 mm German P38s. They no longer relied on horses; the ranger station in Flagstaff had two 1916 Model T Fords then. The outlaws had started using Thompson tommy guns and faster getaway vehicles.

One day, the Flagstaff office got wanted posters for John Hamilton, Russell Clark, Charles Makley, and Henry Copeland, all members of the Dillinger gang. They had been identified by their fingerprints by the FBI identification division and had been flagged with red metal tags indicating they were wanted.

It was not known that they were in a Tucson hotel when a fire broke out there, but three firemen recognized Clark and Makley from their photos. The rangers and the local police took them into custody with John Dillinger and Harry Pier and seized three Thompson machine guns, two Winchester rifles, five bulletproof vests, and $25,000 that had been taken in a Chicago robbery. John Dillinger had a .308 automatic Colt with twenty-rounds clips. The rangers had them all in jail before the rangers' office in Flagstaff even got news of the arrest.

In 1933, the ranger station received three Ford Victorias; one was for Jim's personal use. Their top speed was eighty-five miles an hour, but the roads were so bad that most of the time, they did not go faster than thirty-five miles per hour.

The rangers' office got a new 1935 Ford; it had a bigger trunk and a top speed of a hundred miles an hour. It had a two-way radio, a high-powered .308 Browning Automatic Rifle, a .45 Thompson machine gun, a Winchester shotgun, tear gas, a first-aid kit, red lights, and a siren. The vehicle had Arizona Rangers painted on the front doors.

At that time, Jim was a lieutenant and had more pay, more time off, and more time to spend with the new rangers coming in who were taking the place of those leaving. He was riding an office chair instead of a horse, which he would rather have been doing. He would rather be sleeping out and eating meals cooked over a campfire.

The new rangers were not like the old rangers, who had .45s and would ride for days to bring back lawbreakers often slung over a saddle dead. At that time, they had radios to call for backup or to stop a car. Lawbreakers started having rangers coming out of their ears, and they would give up without a fight. Gone were the old days for Jim. He would receive phone calls and dispatch rangers to handle situations. He would get reports of what happened; nine times out of ten, he would never see a suspect.

Jim and Sara had three children then—one girl and two boys. Jim bought Sara a secondhand 1911 Oakley four-door sedan. Sara did not know how to drive, so Jim took her out to a field and said, "When you learn how to drive, come back here and we'll go home."

One afternoon, a rancher phoned the rangers' office and reported that someone in a big truck had loaded up ten head of his cattle and had driven off with them. Jim asked, "Did you get the truck's license number? What color was it? Did it have any signs on it?"

The rancher replied that he had gotten only the last two numbers of the five-digit Arizona license plate. He said it was brown and had a canvas cover over the back of it, which they realized was to hide the cattle.

Jim said he would send a ranger out to take a report and get some samples of the tire tracks. He told the radio operator to broadcast the information to the patrol cars. He called the sheriff, John Sloan, who said he was a little busy; he asked if the rangers could handle it without him.

Jim agreed to that, and on the way to the ranch, he asked the radio operator to telephone the Navajo police in Window Rock with the information about the theft. Jim was thinking that it would take him only three hours to get to the ranch in his car; in the old days, it would have taken all day on a horse.

The ranger on the scene had made plaster casts of the tire tracks. As the ranger was putting the casts into his patrol car, Jim observed that they were good impressions and said, "These casts will be good evidence at the trial of the rustlers." He asked the rancher if he remembered anything more.

On the way back to Flagstaff, Jim received a radio call— the truck had been found abandoned with no signs of the cattle or the rustlers. The Navajo police were checking the truck for evidence, fingerprints, and residue on the floorboards in the hopes of finding something. Because fingerprinting was fairly new at that time, Arizona did not have a large file, so they would run fingerprints through the FBI's much larger file. The truck was on the other side of Snowflake City, more than a hundred miles away.

Jim told the radio operator that he was going there to look at the abandoned truck and would be out of radio contact. At Holbrook, he turned south on a badly maintained dirt road and was sure he would tear the bottom out of his car. He came across the truck thirty miles farther on. It was a 1932 Reo with solid rubber wheels. Jim was thinking that the driver would have found it difficult to drive on that rough road.

After looking the truck over and making casts of the footprints around the area, he headed back to Flagstaff. He phoned the New Mexico authorities and told them of the rustling and said, "They changed trucks, and there's no information at this time on the vehicle they're using. Do you have casts of other truck tires?"

By the time he got back to Flagstaff, it was ten at night. Sara made coffee and warmed up his supper. The two sat at the kitchen table and talked about the day's events, the children, and their homework. Jim hugged Sara and gave her a peck on the cheek. By the time Sara cleaned up the kitchen, washed the dishes, and went to bed, Jim was asleep.

The next morning, he was in the office at seven. There was no news about the missing cattle. Jim told the radio operator, "They'll never find those cattle. They're probably in a slaughterhouse in New Mexico by now. But I could be wrong. The truck was abandoned on the Navajo reservation, and the Navajo police are good trackers. They may turn up something."

Just then, a telegraph came through, and the radio operator was writing down what was being transmitted. It seemed to go on and on; the radio operator needed more paper. Jim went to the roll-up desk for some paper for the operator.

The first part of the message read, "First National Bank of Arizona in Williams was held up, four people stop. Robbers three men and a woman driver in the car stop. Two men armed with .45 caliber Thompson machine guns. Driving a black 1934 four-door Ford. Arizona license plate but did not get a number. Stop. Going east on Highway 66. Heading into Flagstaff. Stop."

The radio operator gave Jim the last half of the message. When he finished reading it, he told the radio operator to put out an all-points bulletin and arranged for two cars to set up a roadblock on Highway 66. The message said, "They are armed and dangerous, so take no chances. They have probably ditched the black Ford for a different car. It will be a fast one, probably not another Ford and not black. I recommend don't take any chances because they are armed and extremely dangerous. Williams is just twenty-nine miles from Flagstaff. The robbery went down at eleven thirty, so we have to have the roadblocks up before noon. It will not hurt for the rangers to have their Thompson machine guns at hand. The Thompson does not have the power to penetrate the sides of a car but may go through the windshield. You should probably have one of the rangers to back you up with the Browning Automatic Rifle, which has the penetrating power you will need."

Jim was telling the radio operator that he was going out to the roadblock when the radio crackled with a voice of a new ranger: "Officer down! We need an ambulance and backup!" The radio operator called the ambulance and the sheriff's department. Jim ran to his car. He turned on the red lights and the siren and raced off. Over the radio, he heard that the bank robbers had shot their way through the roadblock. There was a woman driver with one man in the front and two in the back. He also heard they were in a red two-door Packard with New Mexico license plates.

Jim got to the highway and turned east with his pedal to the metal. He was doing eighty-five as he left Flagstaff city limits on the highway, and the police car could do about ninety-nine miles an hour. He decided to drive at that speed until the engine blew up or he had the bank robbers. He realized that they would have to be at least fifteen miles ahead of him.

As he neared the New Mexico state line, he radioed Gallup and asked if they had a roadblock set up for the bank robbers. Gallup responded, "Yes, we put up a roadblock when we first got word about the bank robbery. We're on the lookout for a red Packard coming through."

Jim turned off the red lights and reduced his speed to fifty miles an hour. He turned onto the Window Rock and Fort Defiance road; he was in radio range, so he could communicate with the others. They had not seen a red Packard but would keep their eyes open for it. Fort Defiance had also not seen a red Packard or any other car all day.

Jim thought that the robbers might have changed cars again or split up. He told himself, *I have to find that car.* When he got to the Navajo police station at Window Rock, he telephoned the Flagstaff rangers' station to get an update. They said that one of the new rangers had died and Ranger David was in hospital. There was no sign of a red Packard or the bank robbers. Jim said, "They couldn't have disappeared into thin air. I'm sure they decided to slow down and look for somewhere to turn off the highway."

That was exactly what had happened. At Leupp Corners, the robbers turned north. In about one and half miles, they got to Angel Ranch and turned into the driveway. The ranch house was about two hundred yards off the road. The woman and the leader of the group knocked on the front door, and when the rancher's wife opened it, they held a gun to her face. The robbers went inside and asked who else lived there. She said only she and her husband lived there and that her husband was out working; he would not be back until dark. The robbers parked the car in the barn, and when the rancher got home that night, they tied him and his wife up.

The next day, they untied them and told them that if either tried to run, the other would be shot. The rancher said, "I have livestock that needs tending to. Can I go to the barn and take care of them?"

"Yes, go ahead, but remember we have your wife. If you do anything wrong, we'll shoot her."

The wife made breakfast—bacon and eggs, flapjacks, coffee, toast, and milk. The rancher came in from the barn with two buckets of milk and said that he needed to separate the milk so he would be using the separator for a while. The robbers asked, "What does the separator do?" The rancher told them that it separated the cream from the milk, and that produced the butter the robbers had eaten on their flapjacks at breakfast.

One of the men said he was from New York City and had never seen a cow before. The rancher said, "If you're still here tonight, you can come with me and milk the cows and feed the livestock."

What the robbers didn't know was that the rancher had a telephone in the barn and had called the ranger station in Flagstaff to report that he and his wife were being held prisoner by a woman and three men.

When they got the message, the rangers called the Navajo police station in Window Rock; they radioed Jim to tell him that the bank robbers had been located. They told Jim to go to Leupp Corners, where other rangers would meet him. Jim estimated he would be there in twenty minutes. The Navajo police suggested that he proceed with only red lights as the siren could be heard from a long way off in the silence of the desert.

When Jim arrived, he was met by Sheriff Sloan and three rangers from the Phoenix office who had been passing through on their way back to Phoenix and who had offered to help in the raid on the Angel Ranch.

The rangers shared their weapons—six Browning Automatic Rifles, three Thompson machine guns, and sidearms. It was noon when his group started the assault on the ranch house. There was very little cover for them on their side of the house. They heard people talking but could not tell where the voices were coming from. The ranger ordered them to shoot tear gas in the windows on three sides of the house. Jim shouted, "We're the Arizona Rangers! The house is surrounded. Come out with your hands above your heads!"

The woman and two men came out with their hands up. That left one bank robber and the two hostages still in the house, which was filling up with tear gas. Jim shouted again, "Come out with your hands up! This is the Arizona Rangers, and we have the house completely surrounded!" Nothing happened. Jim told the others, "Put in two more rounds of tear gas." He was about to shout another warning when they heard a shotgun blast and a man's voice: "We're coming out. Don't shoot!"

The husband and wife came out the kitchen door with their hands up and rags over their faces. The rancher told Jim that he had shot the last man but that he might still be alive as he had only birdshot in his gun. Jim said they would wait till the tear gas had dissipated before going in. He didn't want to take any chances with that man, who had already killed and would kill again.

After fifteen minutes, the tear gas was mostly gone. Two rangers rushed through the front door while four others rushed through the kitchen door. They found the bank robber facedown in the kitchen doorway. A ranger put his Browning Automatic Rifle barrel on the man's head, but there was no response. One of the robber's hands was exposed, but the other hand was under his body; the rangers thought he might have had a gun in that hand. They trained their guns on him and turned him over. He was indeed holding a gun, but he was dead.

Jim took the gun and informed the rangers outside that it was all over. They put the woman in the back of a police car with a ranger next to her. The two men went in separate cars each with a ranger.

The rangers from the Phoenix office who had stopped by the office were thanked for their help. They said, "Anytime we can help, we will. We're all rangers, and it's our duty to pitch in and help when needed."

Jim went to the hospital to check on Dave. He had .45 caliber bullet holes in his arm and hand. He was in a stable condition, but the doctor wanted to keep him in the hospital for a day or so.

On the way back to his office, Jim stopped by the sheriff's office to thank him. Back at his office, Jim spent the rest of the morning doing paperwork and talking to the radio operator. At noon, he went home for lunch. He and Sara chatted about the day and the children, and by one, Jim was back in his office.

The FBI had come to see about the federal bank robbery; Jim released the prisoners to them. The FBI informed him that murder was not a federal crime, so after the robbers had done their time for the bank robbery, they would be turned over to Arizona to stand trial on five counts of murder; charges had to be filed by the State of Arizona.

After a while, Jim's life got back to the old, boring, daily routine of dealing with Saturday-night drunks and fender benders. Many were passing through on their way to California; they were leaving the dustbowl behind. He was sure that in 1931 and 1932, ten to fifteen families passed through daily in old cars and trucks that were so run-down that Jim wouldn't have used one to go to the store.

The travelers were driving halfway across the United States from Kansas, Missouri, Oklahoma, and Texas. Banks had foreclosed on their farms, and they were going to California to start new lives. Jim had seen some coming back the other way broke and down in the dumps. Jim felt sad when he saw their hardship, but Flagstaff did not have the resources to care for them. Gas cost only 10¢ a gallon, but that was a lot for them.

Jim hated his office job and all the new things—telephones, telegraphs, cars, and rangers who were getting younger every year. He longed for the good old days, but he knew they were gone forever. He really had no complaints; the rangers had treated him well. He was forty-five then and had been an Arizona ranger for twenty-four years. He was a captain and in charge of the Flagstaff ranger station. His pay was good, and he got a new car every year.

Jim and Sara's children were in school, and Sara had more free time. She became a member of a quilting group; the members would gather at someone's house to make quilts, have tea, and chat. Their house was not new, but it was a good house. When they had first moved in, theirs was one of only two houses on their block, but by then, it was full of houses—the city had grown up around them.

That summer, the Flagstaff office received two new Fords with overdrive, red lights, and sirens; they could do more than a hundred miles an hour. The station then had four patrol cars. There were two sergeants—one worked in the outback and was gone for long periods of time—and fifteen privates. Because the office was too small, they moved to a bigger building with the jail on the second floor. Jim was pleased with the new station, which did not have wood floors or a potbelly stove for heating the place and making coffee; they had a new electric coffeepot that kept coffee hot all day, but Jim did not think it tasted as good as coffee made on a wood-burning potbelly stove.

He took one ranger off his customary long assignments and put him in a patrol car. The ranger was mad; he did not like his new assignment, and Jim could relate to that.

One night, Sara told Jim that she wanted to visit her two brothers and a sister in Pennsylvania and meet their children. Her parents had passed away; her mother had died when she was eight. Jim agreed with the plan; the children were out of school, and the weather was good. He felt he needed a vacation himself.

He covered his car's red lights, but his doors still had Arizona Ranger on them. When they set off for Pennsylvania that July, the temperature was over a hundred. They stopped in Albuquerque for dinner and drove to Tucuman, New Mexico, where they planned to stop for the night. However, they drove on to Oklahoma City and arrived after ten that night.

The next day, the family drove through the Ozarks. The weather was warm and dry, and the green, heavily wooded mountains were beautiful. They stopped at a roadside apple cider stand where Jim bought the children small bottles of cider and a gallon of cider for himself and Sara.

Jim was drinking the cider as he drove and was becoming increasingly happy. Concerned, Sara took a drink of the cider and realized it had turned hard—Jim was getting drunk. She told him to pull over; she would handle the driving for a while.

They stopped in St. Louis that night, in Danville, Illinois, the next night, and in St. Mary's, Pennsylvania, the night after that. Sara's family lived on a farm out of town, and it was noon by the time they got there. There were picnic tables set up outside; their family enjoyed meeting after such a long time. Sara did not recognize her older brother as he had changed so much; he had to introduce himself.

They stayed for two days and three nights, and as they said goodbye, both brothers said they would visit her in Arizona one day, but Sara knew in her heart that she would never see them again. She kissed her older sister and cried when she had to say goodbye to her family.

The only problem the family encountered on their journey back home was a flat tire. It took longer to get the spare tire out of the trunk than it did to change the flat because they had to take all their luggage out first.

The closer they got to Flagstaff, the hotter it got. By the time they got home, the temperature was 105. Sara opened all the windows, and they all unpacked the car. The boys went to the front porch and swept up the sand.

The next day, Jim reported back to duty. He looked at the flyers and new wanted posters and asked the radio operator for any news he should know about. The operator told him that there was nothing to report; all had been quiet while Jim has been away. He suggested that perhaps Jim should go on vacation more often.

He was in his office drinking coffee when the phone rang. Jim answered, "Arizona Rangers, Flagstaff office. How can I help you?"

It was the deputy sheriff. "Has anyone told you there are some very bad people with guns coming our way?"

"No," said Jim. "This is the first I've heard about it. Who are they? How many? What weapons?"

Sheriff Sloan came on the line and told Jim he had just received a call from the sheriff's office in Kingman, Arizona. A car full of men had shot up their police cars and lots of windows on the main street. They were driving a late-model black sedan with California plates, but no one had gotten the number.

Jim said, "I'll get my radio operator to send out an all-points bulletin. I'll set up a roadblock on the bridge leading into town."

He wasn't sure when the police cars and windows had been

shot up or when the gunman had left Kingman, which was 145 miles, at least two hours, from Flagstaff. He had a roadblock set up in less than an hour. He was not going to let the game blast their way through a roadblock as had happened before.

He gave instructions to the people manning the roadblock: "Those with BARs are to set up a crossfire pattern. The officers with Thompson machine guns must remember that their guns don't have good penetration or stopping power, so when the time comes for a showdown, don't go rushing in. We're all professional lawmen and don't want any slipups. Smith, take an unmarked car two miles down the highway and keep a lookout. Call on the radio if you see anything, but don't engage with them or try to stop them."

At around three, Smith radio Jim: "I think the party we're looking for just passed me. They're in a black, 1936, four-door sedan license 26336."

Jim told the man at the roadblock, "They're coming. Lock and load."

The car slowed down as it came to the roadblock and went onto the bridge. After the outlaws' car was on the bridge, two rangers drove in behind them and block the bridge. With the heavy-duty equipment in front of them, the outlaws had nowhere to go. They came to a stop in the middle of the bridge. All four doors opened. The gunman put their weapons on the bridge's side barrier and put their hands over their heads. "We give up."

A ranger stepped from behind the bulldozer and told the outlaws to walk away from the car and put their hands on top of the bridge rail. All four of them did.

Other rangers with guns pointed at the outlaws approached with care. Each outlaw was searched, cuffed, and put in different police cars. They were taken to the station and put in cells. The next day, sheriff's deputies came for them and put them in handcuffs and leg irons.

That was the last action the Arizona Rangers were involved in; soon after, the rangers was disbanded. It was only six years later that the rangers were reestablished and are still operating today, but at the time, after thirty-five years with the rangers, Jim was out of work.

Sheriff Sloan decided to retire; he had gotten old and had told Jim that he planned to move to Florida for the weather. Elections for the position of county sheriff were coming up, and many people asked Jim, "Why don't you run for sheriff? You'd be sure to win. You have the know-how, and you need a job."

Jim spoke about it with Sara, and she asked him if that was something he wanted to do. Jim answered, "I don't know. I might just try for sheriff. I'd have to cover a much smaller area, but I'd have just two deputies to help out."

CHAPTER 4

The sheriff's department was much smaller than the Arizona Rangers' department, and it had less funding and older equipment. Jim had to use his own car and did not get paid for mileage, and the pay was less than what he needed. But he was sheriff from 1936 to early 1942, and he had two good deputies who had been with Sheriff Sloan.

Sara and the children were happy that they did not have to move and could keep their house in Flagstaff, which they had rented for many years.

Jim's job was not too different from his previous one with the rangers. The area he had to cover was much smaller than before as he was responsible for just the county, not the whole state. Of course there were the usual Saturday-night drunks and some fights but nothing that required hospital visits.

At the beginning, everything was calm, but because the ranger station was not there anymore, Jim was concerned that he would not have their support in times of trouble. However, the only time he was called out during the first two months was because two ranchers had gone to war over water rights.

At ten thirty one day, he got a call that the ranchers were fighting. Jim told one of the deputies, "I'm going to the Williams ranch." He retrieved a twelve-gauge, double-barreled shotgun and went to the ranch.

He pulled into the yard, and the Williams boy met him; he told Jim that his father and the neighbor were fighting over river water for the cattle. The boy had a horse saddled for Jim, so the two of them rode down to the river. As they rode, Jim asked the boy why they were fighting over water as the water was enough for herds double the size of theirs. The boy answered, "I don't know. I just know they're mad at each other."

When they arrived at the river, Jim shouted, "Hey, you too crazy ranchers! Stop all this nonsense. Put your shotguns up and act like human beings. This is Sheriff James Logan, and if there's any more shooting, it'll be me doing it."

The ranchers came out of their hiding places and walked toward Jim shotguns in hand. Jim asked, "What are you two nuts fighting about? You have enough water here to water ten times the number of cattle you have, but if you want more water, damn the river and create a nice pond."

The ranchers agreed that making a dam would be a good idea. Jim told them to go home and stop fighting. Mr. Williams, the boy, and Jim went back to the ranch house, and Jim drove back to his office. That was the most excitement he had for the month.

An average day for Jim was to go to the office in the morning to read the night report and check for any new flyers or wanted posters. Then he would go down the street to a cantina and have coffee with business friends to get all the latest gossip, and those men were worse gossipers than those in Sara's quilting party were. He would go home for a two-hour lunch break and go back to the office to handle anything that needed his attention. He was bored out of his mind. If he was ever required to put up a roadblock, he wouldn't have the manpower or the weapons to do so. He could not ask the county council for the funds to bring the sheriff's department up to even basic standards; that would have cost $10,000.

The other problem was that he had to use his own car as his deputies used the one police car. Highway 66 didn't have that many people migrating from Oklahoma and Texas as they had during the Great Depression, but vagrants did pass through. It was the sheriff's job to keep them from stopping in his county.

Sara was content with their house; it was old, but it was clean and in good shape. The children were all during well in school though there were times when Jim would have to pull the boys up for their rough playing. Of course, he had playtime tea with his daughter. The previous Christmas, they had given her a kitchen set. The stove had a light that came on when it was turned on, and she would turn the stove on and pretend to make tea and pour it into empty cups. Then she would add make-believe sugar and cream. Jim would pretend to drink the tea and eat the cookies or cakes.

Sara told him, "If one of your deputies were to walk in while you were having tea with your daughter, you'd never live that down!" But Jim just laughed and told his daughter, "That was delicious tea. How about another cup?"

One day, Jim got a telegram warning of a felon whose home was in Flagstaff; he was being released. It was just a heads-up. The man had served twenty years for armed robbery. Jim thought that perhaps he we just an old man who wanted to come home, but he decided to keep a lookout for him and wait and see.

This was the biggest news he had received in the six months

he had been the county sheriff. He bought a new 1939 Oldsmobile that did not have a siren or red lights and was unmarked, so Jim had a siren, red lights, and two spotlights installed. The siren was under the hood, and the red lights were not visible when they were turned down.

One night when Jim was coming home, Sara was having a quilting party. He was tired and did not want to disturb the women, so he went back to the office and went to bed in a cell.

At one in the morning, a deputy brought in a drunk and put him in jail, so Jim drove home. Sara asked him where he had been, and Jim explained the matter. Sara said she was sorry that the quilting party had lasted for so long; everyone had been happy and was having fun.

Sara told Jim that they had finished their quilts Tourists coming through on Highway 66 paid big money for homemade items, and Sara had once sold one for $150, enough for groceries for a year.

When Jim had been sheriff for over a year, he asked Sara where she would like to go on vacation when school was out. Sara said, "I don't know. I always wanted to see San Francisco, so maybe we could go there?"

When the time for their vacation rolled around, they loaded up the Olds and headed for California for two weeks. They got to their hotel and went sightseeing. They went to see the Golden Gate Bridge, which was almost completed then, and then to the ocean. There was a big entertainment center there, and the kids all had fun going on the rides. From there, they went down the road to the Cliff House, where they had dinner and watched the seals on seal rock.

The next day, they took the ferry to Oakland for the day. None of them had been on a ferry before, so they enjoyed the experience. On the third day, they went to the zoo and then to

Fisherman's Wharf. They picked out crabs and dropped them into boiling water to cook. They drove past all the docks and looked at the big ships that would be going all over the world. The two weeks went past fast; at the end, everybody was tired and ready to go home. When they got home, the kids told their friends about the ferry and the big entertainment center.

The day after they returned from vacation, Jim went to the office to see what was going on. There was nothing new; "Same ol' same ol'" the deputy on duty said.

But at five minutes to six on Friday, November 12, 1939, the sheriff's office received a silent alarm from the First National Bank. Jim radioed the police cars and told them to converge on the bank. Jim and the radio operator went to the bank. In front of the bank was a black 1937 Ford with the engine running and someone behind the wheel. When two police cars blocked the driver's escape, he gave up without a fight but would not say how many people were in the bank. Jim went across the street to the bakery and telephoned the bank. The president of the bank answered. When Jim asked him what was going on, he did not answer. Jim said. "Just answer yes or no. Is there someone in the bank?"

"Yes."

"Is it a robbery?"

"Yes."

"How many robbers are there? Four?"

"Yes, that's right."

"Four armed men?"

"Yes, you're right. Goodnight." The president hung up.

Jim went across the street where his deputy was talking to some witnesses outside the bank and told him that there were four armed men in the bank. He asked the deputies to set up a crossfire with their Thompson machine guns. The sheriff's department had only one .306 Browning Automatic Rifle. Jim said, "I'll give them a warning to lay down their weapons and surrender. If they do, I'll tell them we won't kill them. But they will surely try to kill us." Jim hollered into the bank, "The bank is surrounded! Come out with your hands over your head and no one will get hurt!"

When there was no response, Jim shouted again telling the robbers to come out with their hands up. Still no response. They shot two cans of tear gas into the bank, and still got no response from inside. It was a typical standoff; the law enforcement officers were not going in; the robbers would have to come out or die. Getting away was not an option.

All hell broke loose. The four bank robbers rushed out of the door with guns blazing. Jim shouted, "Fire!" The deputies with the Thompson machine guns killed all of them. They took pictures of the whole crime scene and marked all the bullets holes and empty cartridges. They had blocked off the area using the two deputies' police cars and Jim's Olds. When the bank robbers had rushed out shooting wildly, they put bullet holes in all three cars and broke the windshield of one of the deputy's car. One police car had five bullet holes in it. The big glass window of the bakery across the street was shot out, and the front of the bank had numerous bullet holes in it. The next day, the FBI along with the state police came to gather evidence.

After that, everything calmed down again. Saturday-night drunks and some shoplifting at the hardware store were about all Jim and his deputies had to deal with. It was too much of a routine for Jim. He got into his Oldsmobile and cruised down the main street, onto Highway 66, out of town to the county line, and came back. He thought about how he could support his family doing something else. Just then, a new Cadillac went flying past him going over a hundred miles an hour.

Jim turned on his siren and red lights and went after him. They were headed to Flagstaff, so Jim radioed ahead to set up a roadblock at the bridge. He said they needed to stop a blue 1940 Cadillac with Arizona plates 776590. He warned them that they had less than five minutes before the Cadillac reached the bridge.

When he got near the bridge, he saw one police car blocking the road and the traffic backed up. He realized that this was a bad situation as there was a chance that bystanders could be in danger. Jim slowed down to seventy miles an hour and shouted into the radio to open the roadblock. He told them to let the crazy driver through before he killed twenty people.

It seemed that the driver of the speeding vehicle saw that the bridge was blocked and tried to turn but did not make it. The car rolled end to end four times. Jim drove into the field were the car lay on its side with all the doors closed. The police car that had been blocking the bridge arrived soon afterward, and the deputy said that he had called an ambulance. When they opened the doors, they saw a mangled and bloodied person in the driver's seat and some people in the back seat. They could not see how many people there were, but they appeared to be dead. The ambulance arrived, and the medics pronounced three dead at the scene; they took the driver to the hospital, where the doctor said his prospects were not good.

He stationed a deputy outside the driver's room with orders that no one except the medical staff could go in. On his way home, Jim noted that his brakes were not as good as they should have been, so the next morning after seeing the children off to school and kissing Sara goodbye, he drove to the Oldsmobile dealer and had their mechanic look at the brakes. The mechanic told him that he had crystallized the brake shoes by braking at high speeds. "Can you fix it?" he asked. "Yes I can," the mechanic said. "I'll replace the brake shoes."

Jim looked at the 1941 Oldsmobiles and Pontiacs but didn't know then that there would be no '42, '43, or '44 models because of World War II. The company built tanks, not cars, during that time.

Jim was at the bus station when one young man went off to war. He thanked God his boys were too young to be drafted, and Jim was too old to be drafted; his gray hair and wrinkled skin made him look older than he was.

One night at Willy's bar, a knockdown, drag-out fight broke out. A big, two-hundred-pound Indian was raising hell and tearing up everything. When the deputy got there, he did not rush in. Jim arrived shortly afterward, and seeing the situation, he asked the deputy for his baton. Jim went into the crowd swinging the club and hitting people on their shins. He left a trail of drunks lying on the floor and holding their legs. When he got to the Indian, he hit him on the shin, punched him in the stomach, and kicked him in the face. The Indian went down and stayed down.

Jim gave the baton back to the deputy and drove back to the station, where he waited for the deputy to bring the drunk to jail. It was just another Saturday night in Flagstaff—nothing to write home about. Jim has been sheriff for three years, and the novelty had worn off. He did not like all the paperwork and sitting around all day with nothing to do. He felt he was just moping around the house and the office.

One day when he and Sara were talking about the days before cars, he said, "I believe that was a better time to live. Now, everything has to be done quickly. Do you remember when we met? It had taken me over a week on horseback to get there. Then when the train came through, the time was cut down to four hours on the train and five hours on horseback. Now, we could drive it in two hours. How I love that redheaded schoolmistress!"

Sara told him that the first time she had laid eyes on him, she thought he was a tall drink of water.

That Sunday after church, Jim was sitting on the porch when around the corner of the house came Sara driving a two-team horse and buckboard. She came to a stop in front of Jim and asked, "Are you new in town, stranger? Climb aboard!" She drove out of town and down to the river. They tied up the horses in the shade near the water, and Sara spread out a blanket and the contents of a picnic basket.

Jim was thinking how nice it was to be out in the open like that; he thought it was almost as good as camping out on the trail in the good old days. But he enjoyed the picnic and especially Sara's company. He asked her, "Do you fool around on the first date?"

"Sometimes," she replied.

The sun was going down by the time Sara drove back home in her old Oakley after returning the horses and buckboard. As she got home, the phone rang. It was David, the deputy, who needed Jim's help. Jim put on his uniform, got in the Olds, hit the red lights, and sped to the office. He asked what the emergency was. It was a Sunday evening, and all should have been quiet.

Deputy David said he had received a call from Willows that someone had blown the front doors off the bank but had not managed to blow open the safe; they had left empty-handed. They had no description of the people involved or how many they were.

Jim said, "They must be amateurs because two sticks of dynamite in the right place would've opened that bank vault like a can opener would open a can. We don't know what they look like, and we don't know who they are, so what do the people at Willows want us to do? We can sit on the highway and look at people as they pass, but that's not going to do much good. If they're amateurs, they might take a shot at the police car. I don't think they would be that dumb, but maybe they are. Who knows?

This is nonsense. I'll call the Willows constable and see if he has any more information. If he doesn't, I'm going home to bed."

The constable told him that there had been no witnesses but that his mechanic had said he had heard the getaway car, which sounded like it had a V-8 engine, and it might have been a Ford. The constable could not give them any more information, so Jim said, "I'm too old and too tired to chase shadows. I'll put a patrol car on the side of the highway in hopes that the amateurs will panic when they see it. I'll come by tomorrow when it's light and look the place over. It's a federal bank, so you should contact the FBI."

When Jim got back home, Sara asked about the emergency, and Jim told her what he knew. Sara was puzzled at that because Willows was a small town with a very small bank and would have had very little money in it. "Well, it takes all kinda nuts to make a fruitcake," said Jim.

In 1942, the election for sheriff was coming up. Jim told the city council that he would not stand for reelection, and he recommended Deputy Sheriff DJ Hamilton for the position. On December 7, 1941, of course, everything had changed, and David had volunteered for the army. He was called up but was rejected due to injuries in his arm he had sustained when he was shot in the line of duty.

But Jim changed his mind and agreed to stand for reelection because all the men were joining the armed forces. He was reelected county sheriff for four more years. His old Oldsmobile was about to fall apart; everything on it had been repaired or replaced. Sara said, "I was wondering what we were going to do if you were no longer the sheriff."

"Well, with the war and all the young men in the service, I felt it was my duty to carry on as sheriff for the duration. So I'll be sitting around doing nothing for four more years. That's what the sheriff does—sit in his office and wait."

Jim hated having to go out to the highway and pick up parts of victims who had been killed or were badly hurt. It seemed it got worse every year as the cars got faster. On prom night in 1939, two cars with eight kids were in an accident. He knew one of the girls because she had come to his house to see his kids. They picked one girl up with sponges and put her remains in a shoe box.

Then there was also always some nut who thought he could outrun the police. Jim thought, *He might outrun my old car, but he can't outrun my two-way radio. I can call ahead and have a police car stop him farther down the road.* There would always be the Saturday-night drunks being taken to jail, but all in all, the job was just sitting and waiting.

In 1942, the US Army established a prisoner of war camp ten miles southeast of Flagstaff. That meant that Flagstaff had to supply a police officer to guard prisoners when they needed to be taken to the hospital or elsewhere. When they picked up a prisoner from the camp, they handcuffed him and fastened the cuffs to a chain around his waist that connected to a chain that went to his ankle cuffs. All that had to be in place before the prisoner could leave the camp. Some of the German prisoners could speak better English than Jim could. Very few prisoners were dangerous or tried to escape; most were content to sit the war out, but some were true Nazis who would try anything to escape or interrupt the daily routine.

In 1943, Jim heard talk about reestablishing the rangers; if that was the case, he would go to the headquarters in Phoenix and see about being included. In the last part of 1944, the state legislators voted to reestablish the new Arizona Rangers as they are known today. When they were reestablished in World War II, there was a shortage of manpower due to the war. The rangers offered him the same pay as a captain, but he was not in command of a station; his new job would be in Phoenix training new rangers.

When Jim explained that he had to finish his term as county sheriff in Flagstaff, he was told that that would not be a problem; he could report to the Phoenix training center after his term was up.

Jim returned to Flagstaff and told Sara about the offer. He completed his term as sheriff. He was given two more deputies to help with the transportation of the prisoners of war. He had no trouble other than the usual Saturday-night drunks. During the war, people had ration cards for food and gasoline, but the sheriffs' cars had A-class ration cards for gas.

To Jim, it seemed that all the bad guys were in the service— there were no cattle rustlers or bank robbers and very few speeding vehicles because gas was rationed.

CHAPTER 5

Jim agreed with the terms he had been offered. The rangers gave him the rank and salary of a captain due to his forty-five years' experience. He was to report to the Phoenix training school just south of the city limits by the beginning of the year. That gave him more than ninety days to get moved and set up their new household. It meant putting the children in a new school in the middle of the year, which was not a good time for them. The family had lived in Flagstaff for so long; it would be hard to leave friends behind, but Jim knew that Sara and the children would adapt quickly.

They found a nice, three-bedroom ranch-style place on a big plot for reasonable rent. When Jim checked in, he received a new captain's uniform. He thought it was dumb, but he just cussed under his breath about it and put it on. There were no recruits at the school yet, so Jim had a chance to meet the other instructors and study the courses he was to teach.

One Monday morning, a Greyhound bus pulled up in front

of the administration office and recruits came pouring out. The sergeant at arms got them all lined up and facing in the same direction, which impressed Jim to no end.

On Wednesday when they got to Jim's classroom, the recruits were all in new uniforms, behaving well, and paying attention to what he said. They carried no sidearms. Jim discovered that he liked to teach, and all was going well—he had no complaints.

His children were happy in their new school, and Sara was ecstatic about their new home. There were no bad guys shooting at her husband, and there were no long days for him. The last class finished at four o'clock, so he had time to do his homework before going home at five.

Jim saw that some of the students had problems he could assist them with, and they all wanted to hear the old ranger's stories about horses, Colt .45s, and eating beef jerky and hardtack around a campfire. Jim was in hog heaven telling stories about the old days. He told them that his schooling consisted of going after outlaws; rangers who brought them back without getting killed passed the test. James Logan, an old, over-the-hill Arizona ranger was teaching recruits.

His two boys, Jim Junior and Bob, and his daughter, Mary Lou, would catch the bus to school right outside their house. While Sara had to hurry the boys to catch the bus, Mary Lou liked school very much and was always eagerly waiting for the bus to arrive. The children learned to speak Spanish from their classmates.

On his way home, Jim used to pass a tractor that was for sale. It had sat there for four months or so. One evening, Jim stopped at the farmhouse and asked about the tractor; it was a five-year-old New Holland 170 with a bucket on the front and a rototiller on the back. Jim bought it for $400; the farmer said he would get his workers to load it on a truck and bring it to Jim's house.

Jim figured out why the farmer had sold it; the tractor was a diesel with glow plugs that had to be heated up before the tractor could be started. When the farmer's farmhands had tried to start it, they did not hold the key for long enough for the glow plugs to get hot enough to ignite the fuel and therefore had trouble starting it, but Jim never had trouble with it. The rototiller was great for weeding their ten acres most of which they didn't use. The boys would take turns driving the tractor as well.

After the recruits had taken their first test, Jim would identify the lowest men on the totem pole and personally tutor them; sometimes that worked and sometimes it didn't, but Jim kept trying. He remembered his graduating class of rangers; half of them had been killed due to their stupidity. Classes would graduate, and new recruits would come. The war was over, and the soldiers were coming home. Some of the ranger recruits were young men fresh out of the military and looking for a good, solid job with decent pay.

After the war, car companies started making cars once more. Jim's Oldsmobile was on its last legs, so he bought a Pontiac Fire Chief. The new car was much lighter than the Olds and had a whole lot more get up and go. They were no red lights, sirens, or symbols, just a sticker in the back window reading Arizona Ranger Instructor Parking Permit 1102. That sticker kept him from being stopped for speeding. Sara said she also wanted a new car, so they picked out a Ford club coupe in two-tone green.

One Saturday, Jim was invited to play golf with other instructors. He had never played golf, but he played that day and a few other times. However, that was the end of his golfing career. He decided he would rather stay at home with the family than chase a little white ball around the golf course.

When he turned sixty-five, he had been an instructor for over five years, and he began thinking about putting in for retirement.

He had been with the rangers for a total of thirty-five years. His retirement pay and his Social Security pay together would be about half of what he was earning, but he thought they could get by on that. The boys would be starting college, but the ranger wouldn't pay for their college.

One Friday afternoon, a young lad came into the backyard when Jim was working in the garden. He said, "Good afternoon, Mr. Logan. My name is Richard Galloway. Mary Lou and I go to school together and sometimes sit at the same table at lunch. We talk and laugh and have a good time enjoying one another's company. I'm here to ask your permission to take Mary Lou to the movies this Saturday."

That set Jim back on his heels. His daughter was only sixteen but had boys calling on her. Jim asked Richard, "What movie is showing? What time does it let out? How are you going to get to the movies and back?"

"I have a driver's license. My dad will let me use the family car."

"Have you asked Mary Lou if she wants to go to the movies with you?"

"I wanted to ask your permission first."

Jim went in the house and told her why the lad was there. Sara said, "I've met Richard before when he came visiting after school. The two boys like him."

Jim said, "But Mary Lou is so young to be dating."

Sara said that it was Jim's decision; she would support him in whatever he decided. Coming out into the backyard, she said, "Hello, Richard," and sat beside him. Mary Lou came out, and Richard took her hand and asked her if she wanted to go to the movies with him on Saturday. Mary Lou said yes.

Damn! Jim thought. *Am I that old that my baby girl is going on a date?* He remembered his and Sara's first date, a picnic off the back of a buckboard when Sara was twenty-two and Jim was twenty-seven—not like the kids of that time. If the boys had girlfriends, Jim did not know anything about it. They were nineteen and twenty-one; Jim assumed that they kept matters like that to themselves. They both had jobs and were gone all day. Both had weekends off, and they both had cars that they had paid for. Jim paid the insurance on all four of their cars.

On Saturday afternoon, a nicely dressed Richard arrived in his dad's car, which looked as if it had just come off the showroom floor. Jim was sure Richard had spent all morning cleaning it up. Jim invited him in and told him Mary Lou would be down shortly.

Richard was sitting on the couch when Mary Lou came downstairs. He stood and said, "You look nice, Mary Lou. Are you ready to go?"

Mary Lou said yes, and they walked to the door. Richard opened the door for her, and when they got to the car, he opened the door for her and helped her in. They drove off, and Jim watched them through the window until they were out of sight.

Sara said, "Jim, don't worry about them. Mary Lou's a good girl, and you don't have anything to worry about her."

Bob, the youngest son, said, "I don't know, Dad. If she were my daughter, I'd worry. What if their horse becomes lame and they have to shoot it? Mary Lou might be a little late coming home from the matinee."

Sara said, "Leave your father alone. Stop making fun of his old-fashioned ways."

Jim said, "In all the time I rode horses, I never had a flat tire."

Jim Junior said, "You're right, Dad, but what was the top speed on that horse?"

Sara said, "Okay, enough! You boys leave your dad alone."

Jim went out to rototill their acres for a few hours. He came in, washed his hands, and put his dirty clothes in the laundry basket. He drank coffee sitting in the kitchen in his underwear and stocking feet.

Mary Lou came into the kitchen and said, "Dad, thanks for allowing me to go to the movies. It was a good movie, and Richard is fun to be with."

"Does this mean you two will be going to the movies again?"

"I don't know. Perhaps," Mary Lou said.

Sara said, "All you people get out my kitchen if you want to eat tonight. It's time for me to start dinner." Mary Lou helped her mother prepare the food while Jim and his sons listened to the Amos 'n' Andy show on the radio; Jim sat in his favorite chair that everyone knew was his and would not sit in. After the show, the Green Hornet came on, and in the middle of that show, Sara called them for their meal. As they sat at the table, Jim thought about how wonderful it was to have his family all around him.

On Monday morning, Jim put on his uniform and drove to the academy, which was three miles away. It was time for midterm exams, so he graded exam papers. There was no one in that class that he would remember.

At noon, he went to the cafeteria for coffee and a sandwich. The shooting range instructor was there, and Jim asked him if he received hazardous-duty pay. The instructor said he did not but that his job wasn't too bad—nobody had tried to shoot him yet.

Jim had just one class that afternoon, so he hung around the cafeteria for longer than usual. After that, he went to the instructors' lounge and had more coffee before going to set up the classroom for his next class. After class, the students asked Jim about the good old days, and Jim told them about chasing the cattle rustlers who had killed High Pockets. He did not tell them that he would have liked an excuse to shoot the rustlers. After all that time, High Pocket's murder still made him mad.

After the group left, Jim finished his paperwork and drove

home. He felt that he was just marking time until retirement. The life he had loved as a ranger had gone forever.

When he pulled into the driveway, he saw a car he did not recognize. He went inside and saw Mary Lou and Richard sitting on the couch. Richard stood and said, "Good afternoon, sir." Mary Lou said hi to her father.

Jim went to the kitchen and asked Sara how long their meeting had been going on. Sara said, "For some time now. If Richard cannot use their family car, he comes to our house on the school bus with Mary Lou."

Jim and Sara talked about how old they felt now that their baby daughter was dating. Jim would have liked to stop the romance. Sara told him that it was just puppy love and that in time the romance would end.

Jim Junior came home from work, said hi to his father, and kissed his mother on the cheek. He asked, "Are Richard and Mary Lou in the parlor again?"

Jim asked, "What do you mean again?"

Jim Junior poured a cup of coffee and sat at the kitchen table with his father. "Take the blinders off, Pop. Mary Lou's a teenager and is doing what teenagers do."

"Not my daughter," Sara said. "Mary Lou's a good girl. She won't do anything wrong, so just sit back and relax and let them have their fun. I asked Richard to come to church with us on Sunday, and he said he would."

When Bob came home from work, he warned Mary Lou that Richard should leave before their dad saw them together. Mary Lou told him that he had seen them together on the couch.

After Richard left, the family had dinner. Jim told the boys, "Mary Lou's bringing her boyfriend to church on Sunday. Why don't you boys bring your girlfriends?"

Jim Junior said his girlfriend was Catholic; he didn't know

if she would come to his church, but he said he would ask her. Bob said that if his girlfriend went to church, the church would probably fall down, but he said he would ask her. That was the first time the boys had ever mentioned anything about having girlfriends.

On Sunday morning, Sara, Jim, Mary Lou, and Richard went to church and saw Bob and his girlfriend, but Jim Junior's girlfriend had gone to her own church. When Bob did not introduce his girlfriend, she said, "Hello, Mr. and Mrs. Logan. My name is Ginger, and I've been seeing your son for about a year now."

Bob did not say anything, but Jim Junior said, "Hello, Ginger. I'm glad to meet you."

All seven went into the church and sat together. After church, Jim suggested that they have dinner at a new drive-in restaurant. The kids were all keen on that idea, but Sara was worried about where the food had come from and how it had been prepared. Jim said they would never know unless they went to see for themselves.

At the drive-in restaurant, they saw through the window into the kitchen where hamburgers and french fries were being cooked. Sara watched for a little while and said that she thought it would be all right to eat there.

After that, they went home and had a relaxing Sunday. Jim changed out of his Sunday suit into his work clothes and went out to till their acres. About five thirty, he went inside for some coffee. He sat in his chair and read the newspaper.

On Monday morning, he went to the academy and thought some more about retiring. His job bored him, but he was not sure what he would do after he retired. The recruits had taken their finals and were close to graduating. One recruit asked Jim to tell them about the old days—when it was just him and the bad guys. Jim, who loved telling stories, told them about one of his adventures.

"One time, I had to go after someone who had killed nineteen people. I rode for six days on horseback to get to the town where he was. I found him playing cards in a saloon."

He told them that by the time he had taken care of his horse, had some dinner, and found a room for the night, the killer had gotten word that a ranger was in town looking for him. He told the recruits about how that killer had tried to make him think he would use his Colt Peacemaker on him, but Jim knew he would try to use his belly gun he kept hidden in his vest. Jim said, "I told him I was an Arizona ranger and I was there to take him back to Tombstone. The outlaws said, 'I'm not going anywhere with you, ranger.' He started to pull his smaller gun. I shot him four times. He was dead before he hit the ground." Jim told the recruits that in those days, the best gun was a single-action .44 Colt Peacemaker unlike the double-action .45 automatics they were using then.

He went home and had a pleasant evening with his family; they chatted about their days. Bob had gotten home early because it was slow at work. Jim Junior said that he did the same thing at work every day but that he enjoyed his job. Mary Lou had taken her final exams that day and would learn the results in a week. Sara said she never got lonely with everyone out of the house because she had so much to do.

After dinner, they gathered in the living room and listened to their favorite radio programs—Amos 'n' Andy, the Lone Ranger, and the Shadow—"No one knows what lurks in the hearts of men. The Shadow knows."

Jim wondered how long it would take for the rangers to process his retirement papers so he could stop putting on his uniform and going to a job he didn't like.

At work the next day, he asked the secretary in the administration office whether his papers had arrived. They had not, but she told him she would let him know when they came. Jim said, "Good. You do that. I'm just biding my time until the paperwork comes through, but I have my fishing rod all cleaned and oiled."

He went to his first class, and he was tempted to tell the recruits that they could skip the class and lie on the front lawn in the sunshine. Jim thought they would get as much education doing that as they would listening to him. However, he carried on and instructed the recruits on the legal procedures for taking someone into custody. They almost had to be Philadelphia lawyers to do anything at that time if they shot anyone—that would require a good twenty-four hours of paperwork in duplicate. He told them that even if they just fired their weapon and didn't hit anything, they would still need to fill out the paperwork.

Just before he left for lunch, he was called into the administration office; his retirement paperwork had arrived. With a big smile on his face, he looked over the documents.

During his first afternoon class, he taught the recruits about their power to arrest someone and when to shoot. He warned them that they would have only a split second to decide what they would do. Jim told him they could not let the bad guys win because they might be killed. On the other hand, he said that they had to be very careful about killing innocent people. The discussion got the whole class fired up, and when it was time to end the lesson, the recruits were still asking questions.

After the last student had left the classroom, Jim went home and told Sara that his retirement papers had come in and that he just had to fill them out. He told her that he was too old to go back out into the field and that he did not like being an instructor very much. He would get 59 percent of his pay when he retired, and with his Social Security, they could manage. He said, "I think I'll retire on January 1, 1950. I'll be sixty-eight, and I don't know how many more years I'll have. We need to have fun and enjoy our old age together. Do you want to remain here in Phoenix, or would you rather return to Flagstaff?"

Sara said, "The boys are working here. If we move back to Flagstaff, they'll be out of a job. Plus you know that Mary Lou would have a fit if we even mentioned moving to Flagstaff. I suggest we stay here in Phoenix. Perhaps we should buy a small house on a city lot so we could have city sewer, water, and maybe electricity that won't go out every time it rains. They're building new homes in the northern part of the city. Let's drive over there some weekend and look at them."

Jim said that what they were paying in rent would probably cover the mortgage payments on a new home without the acreage.

When Jim Junior came in from work, Jim started to talk to him about retiring, but Sara suggested he wait until the whole family was together. The family chatted about other things. Jim Junior said his girlfriend wanted him to convert to Catholicism. Bob said he had been given a pay raise; he was then earning four dollars an hour, almost as much as a plumber would earn.

After dinner, Jim said, "What do you kids think about my retiring from the rangers?"

"Dad," Jim Junior said, "you've been in Arizona ranger all my life. It's time for you to retire and for you and Mom to take it easy."

Bob said, "That's great, but what will you do with your time if you aren't working? Will we stay in this house?"

"I'd be happy if we stayed right here," Jim said. "If we move to a new home, I'll kick you boys out. You're both working and making good money. Mary Lou might have to go to a new school. We might just stay here and pay rent for the rest of our lives."

On the day Jim officially retired, they had a ceremony at the ranger academy, and he was given a gold watch and a certificate of retirement.

By July, Jim Junior and his girlfriend were living together. She had told him that she would not marry him until he converted to Catholicism. Bob had a different girlfriend, and they seemed to be getting along quite well. He did not come home every night.

When Mary Lou turned nineteen, she married Richard, who had just turned twenty. Jim told Mary Lou that he thought they were too young to get married, but he gave her some advice: "Remember this. A fight is like playing tennis. If you don't hit the ball back, the game's over. If you don't shout back, the fight's over."

James Logan, who had dedicated forty-nine years to the rangers, passed away on July 21, 1976, at the age of ninety-six and was buried in the Phoenix cemetery. Sara had passed away at the age of seventy-one on October 16, 1966. Jim was buried next to Sara. A double headstone bore their names, dates of birth and death, and the inscription, Together in Heaven for Eternity.

Printed in the United States
By Bookmasters